This is the field where the goats live. There's no grass left and they're hungry. They want to cross the river to the field over there, but they need our help to get past the nasty Troll. Shall we help them?

The goats need to cross this bridge, but the Troll lives underneath and he wants to eat them.

The goats are going to row across the river.
Do you think it's a good idea?

We'd better watch out for the Troll while they're rowing.
If we see him, what are we going to yell?

Oh no, the boat is sinking! They need to get out of there!

That plan didn't work, and where's the Troll?

The goats are going to fly across the river.
Do you think that's a good idea?

We'd better watch out for the Troll.
If we see him, what are we going to yell?

We'd better watch out for the Troll.
If we see him, what are we going to yell?

Oh no! They've landed in the middle of the river!

Those poor goats will have to cross the bridge after all.
Silly Goat is going first. (He must be very silly!)

There's only one goat left. He's big and he's fat but the Troll is much bigger. Do you think he'll reach the other field?

For Odile Josselin, who has supported us
through thick and thin
S.G.

To Jonathan Hinde and David Lynch
P.U.

First published in 2017 by Hodder Children's Books

Text copyright © Sally Grindley 2017
Illustration copyright © Peter Utton 2017

Hodder Children's Books
An imprint of Hachette Children's Group
Part of Hodder & Stoughton
Carmelite House
50 Victoria Embankment
London EC4Y 0DZ

A catalogue record of this book is available from the British Library.

HB ISBN: 978 1 444 93783 1
PB ISBN: 978 1 444 93784 8
2 4 6 8 10 9 7 5 3 1

Printed in China

An Hachette UK Company
www.hachette.co.uk
www.hachettechildrens.co.uk